Bailey BEATS THE BLAH

KAREN TYRRELL

ILLUSTRATED BY

AARON POCOCK

5% of book proceeds will be donated to
Kids Helpline
www.kidshelp.com.au
24/7 support and counselling for young people 5–25 years
Call 1800 55 1800

Published by Digital Future Press 2013

National Library of Australia Cataloguing-in-Publication entry:
A catalogue record for this book is available from the National Library of Australia.

Book cover design and formatting services by BookCoverCafe.com

Tyrrell, Karen
Bailey Beats the Blah
Pocock, Aaron, illustrator
A823.4

www.KarenTyrrell.com

First Edition 2013
ISBN: 978-0-9872740-4-5 (pbk) 978-0-9872740-5-2 (e-bk)

In loving memory

Gloria June Cox

Bailey hated his new school. He buried his head deep into his soft, warm pillow.

Fuzzy slobbered all over Bailey's face.

'**Blah!** Go away, Fuzzy!'

'Come on, Bailey,' Mum said. 'It's time to get up.'

Bailey stared at his homework lying on the desk. 'Mum, my tummy hurts.'

'Bailey, you must go to school today.'

Bailey dragged himself out of bed and tumbled onto the floor. His wobbly legs carried him to the bathroom.

He looked at his sad face in the mirror. **'Blah!'** he said to his reflection.

Bailey slumped over his bowl of rice bubbles. His fruit juice slopped onto his chin.

He clutched at his squirming stomach. 'Mummmm, I really do feel sick.'

Bailey took his shoes outside to put them on. They were his special sneakers with stars and rockets.

He shoved Fuzzy away.
'**Blah!** Leave me alone.'

Bailey trudged down the road to the bus stop. Fuzzy followed him, wagging his tail.

'Go back, Fuzzy. You can't come with me,' said Bailey.

Fuzzy turned to go home.

Bailey heaved himself onto the school bus. He passed all the friends who were chuckling together and plonked down on a seat at the back.

Bailey wished he had a friend.

The bus arrived at school just as the bell rang. Bailey got off the bus after all the other kids.

He forced his legs to shuffle towards the classroom, but they didn't want to go.

Bailey pushed open the door
and stared at the kids inside.

He thought they were all
whispering about him.

He had never felt so unhappy.

Miss Darling came in with a brand new kid. Bailey noticed that the boy's hands were shaking.

'Good morning, class,' said Miss Darling. 'This is Tom. Bailey, can Tom sit next to you?'

23

Bailey moved over so Tom could
sit down.

'Let's write our stories together,'
Bailey suggested.

Slowly Tom began to relax.
Bailey smiled, and Tom smiled too.

At lunchtime, Bailey took Tom around the school.

Bailey wasn't very good at sport. Tom showed him how to dribble the soccer ball ... and score a goal.

After lunch, Bailey and Tom worked on their science project together.

The next morning Bailey's eyes flashed open. He leaped out of bed.

Fuzzy sprang into his arms.

'Tom and I are launching our rocket today,' Bailey told Fuzzy. 'We're going to have a **blast**!'

KAREN TYRRELL was born in Sydney, Australia. From the age of seven she wanted to teach young children. She taught in Sydney and Brisbane primary schools, later teaching classes for gifted and talented children.

Karen has two children of her own, and a bunch of nieces and nephews. Today she writes stories that empower children to connect with their inner happiness and imagination.

Discover more of Karen's mental-health books for children and grownups, as well as FREE activities, downloads, school visits and upcoming events at:

KarenTyrrell.com

CPSIA information can be obtained
at www.ICGtesting.com
Printed in the USA
BVXC01n0027170914
367076BV00004B/6